P9-BYZ-241

TBH, This Is
SO Awkward

Also by Lisa Greenwald

11 Before 12

TBH, This Is SO Awkward

. . . 😬

KATHERINE TEGEN BOOKS
An Imprint of HarperCollins Publishers

LISA GREENWALD

Katherine Tegen Books is an imprint of HarperCollins Publishers.

TBH #1: TBH, This Is So Awkward
Copyright © 2018 by Lisa Greenwald
Emoji icons provided by EmojiOne
Photo on page 45 © 2018 by BW Folsom/Shutterstock
All rights reserved. Printed in the United States of America. No
part of this book may be used or reproduced in any manner
whatsoever without written permission except in the case of
brief quotations embodied in critical articles and reviews. For
information address HarperCollins Children's Books, a division
of HarperCollins Publishers, 195 Broadway, New York, NY 10007.
www.harpercollinschildrens.com

Library of Congress Control Number: 2017934899
ISBN 978-0-06-268990-0 (paper-over-board)
ISBN 978-0-06-268991-7 (pbk.)

Typography by Aurora Parlagreco
19 20 21 22 23   PC/LSCC   10 9 8 7 6

❖
First Edition

For Hazel

BFFAE

CECILY

I know we will c each other @ bus in 3 min but doesn't it feel like we've been out of school for soooooo long ⁉️

Scared 2 go back 😨 😨

GABRIELLE

🐧 Yes! Running late

Hold bus 4 me!!! 🏃

PRIANKA

Already here! Hurry!! 🤍

Sixth-Grade English
New Year's Resolutions

On the back of this page, please write a letter to yourself with your New Year's resolutions. Be as honest as possible. You are the only one who will see it. We will mail it back to you in December so you can see the progress you made over the course of the year.

Good luck and have fun!

Dear Self:

Ummm. This is so awkward. So... what are my New Year's resolutions? Well, I want to do well in school, maybe all A's, even. I also want to make new friends, but still stay friends with my BFFs, Pri and Cece. Maybe I will run for student council or something, too. Wow—this is a lot to do in one year. I'm tired now! OK, bye, Self, LOL!

xoxox Gabs

Gabs. Do you have any clue what Mr. D is talking about? xo Pri   PRI! Literally no clue. :(xoxo Gabs

DOLPHIN SQUAD 🐬🐬🐬

P   C   G

PRIANKA

Sneaking to use fone in 2nd fl b-room

Maybe u will sneak 2 ⁉️

How's 1st day back

CECILY

U sent that text 4ever ago—just got it

We r allowed 2 use phones in sci this sem 📱

Mr. D made special app 4 labs 📱📱📱📱

3

Dear Cecily,

Happy New Year! Hee hee. I have a New Year's goal and a New Year's resolution. My goal is to get the highest average in the grade, and keep up with Ingrid. It's hard having an older sister who is a genius. My resolution is to not get so stressed when big projects are assigned. Also to volunteer more. And maybe convince Mom and Dad that we should adopt a shelter dog.

Love, ME

READING LOG

Hi, Reading Log Partner Gabrielle! My email is: victoriasparkles11@gmail.com and my phone number is 203-555-2792. Bye!

—Victoria

ugh, GABS! i am so mad we aren't reading lab partners this semester. i am stuck with talon corbet! :(xo Pri

I know, Pri!! I think Ms. Marburn split us up on purpose! UNFAIR! xoxox Gabs

Dear Victoria Grace Melford,

My New Year's resolution is to survive this. My parents are the absolute meanest in the entire world to make me move in the middle of the school year. Seriously, who does that? My dad should've just stayed in Philadelphia for the rest of the year. But no, we had to move and now I am stuck here knowing nobody. So yeah, I don't care about New Year's resolutions. I just want to survive this torture.

Sincerely,

Victoria Grace Melford

From: Gabrielle Katz
To: Prianka Basak, Cecily Anderson
Subject: COMPUTER LAB! YAYYY!!!

Hi, girlies!!!!

I'm in Ms. Pinelli's computer lab right now and we're learning how to get our notes and homework off the new school system they installed over break. Do you know it's called Sestina? So fancy! But of course I took a break to email you guys! I LOVE YOUUUUU!!!!! Write back ASAP. Or text. OR see you on the bus!

xoxoxoxoxoxo FOREVER,
Gabs

Dear myself:
Hi, Prianka! How are you? I'm good, Prianka. Nice to hear from you. HAHA! I crack myself up. OK, time for New Year's resolutions! Umm.

Basically my New Year's resolution is to make my bed every day, keep my room clean so Mom doesn't freak, and pretty much be the most awesome girl in the grade.

Love, Prianka

🐘🐘🐘🐘 4EVER

P C G

CECILY

Did we all survive 1st day? Sorry I missed bus ride home but I got the boots! 👢👢👢

GABRIELLE

Barely survived 😫 all this happened

1. Pri & I got caught passing notes in English 🙅

2. Ms. Marburn said to consider it a warning

3. We r reading THE HUNDRED DRESSES 👗👗👗👗👗👗👗👗👗👗👗👗👗👗👗👗

It's Ms. M's fave! YIPPEE 👏👏👏👏

CECILY

Oh so jeal!!! 🙍‍♀️

PRIANKA

Hate how they change scheds each sem

Only 1 study hall now 😠😠😠

CECILY

I don't have any classes w/ M girls this sem, do u

PRIANKA

Just saw them @ lunch

All wore same mint green uneven tee

So matchy matchy 😼😼

GABRIELLE

Ewwww

I didn't see that 🚫🚫

CECILY

Should we match tomorrow

JK 😂 😂

GABRIELLE

LOL 😂

PRIANKA

I gotta start hw

Mom is already nagging me & have Bal Vihar class laterz 📚 📚

CECILY

Mwah 🤍 😘

GABRIELLE

TATA xo

Cece!! U HAVE A BOY BADMINTON PARTNER

GABS!! U R DOING HAND NOTES AGAIN!!!
MY MOM WILL BE SO MAD!!!

ONLY WAY TO PASS NOTES
IN GYM–NO PAPER!

From: Victoria Melford
To: Kimberly Higgins, Nicole Landenor
Subject: MISSING YOU!!

Dear Kim and Nicole:

I miss you guys so much. I am so mad that my parents made us move. Isn't it illegal to make your daughter move schools midyear??? So far my new school is terrible. No one talks to me! I mean, I know it was only the first day. But I had nowhere to sit for lunch. I just sat at the end of a table and ate silently. :(

Can we please plan a sleepover over spring break? Tell me everything that's going on. Maybe I can convince my parents to move back.

xoxo Victoria

Dear Diary,

I like Colin so much. I know you already know this, because, duh, I've written it a million times. I want to tell my friends I like him but I'm so scared. We don't talk about boys like that ever. I wonder if Colin will ever like me. Or if he'll ever know I like him. :(And guess what? Colin is Cecily's badminton partner!!!

Love,
Gabby

 **SQUAD**

P C G

PRIANKA

U guys r never gonna believe this

Remember that kid Vishal who goes 2 Bal Vihar with me

He switched 2 Yorkville from West End 😳 😮 😨

GABRIELLE

R u serious

Midyear ⁉️

☹️

PRIANKA

IDK. My mom said something about a math program here

Pos, he's a math genius ✏️💡

CECILY

Wait just got back from store

R u serious

Kid who played in Little League World Series & u made me watch but he was a benchwarmer ⚾ ⚾ ⚾

PRIANKA

Yes that kid Vishal

Funny, right 😂

CECILY

Totes

Snacks for sat sleepover: soft batch cookies, swedish fish, baked lays, doritos, hershey's miniatures, iced tea, and Sprite

& I can always get more 🌀

GABRIELLE

YUM

Thank u 👍

PRIANKA

YAY SO EXCITED 👏

CECILY

See u 2 mañana 💕 🤍

PRIANKA

Smooches 💋 💋 💋

GABRIELLE

Nighty night 😴 🌙 z^z

READING LOG

Hi, Victoria—Here is my reading log. I only read six pages last night. This is my 1st time reading this book. Have you read it before? How does Wanda stay so calm? If u have questions about my notes, let me know. K bye.

—Gabby

From: Cecily Anderson
To: Gabrielle Katz, Prianka Basak
Subject: Hi from 7th period study hall

Hi, friends!

I'm writing this from study hall. We're allowed to use computers today. Mara had to change her schedule because she got moved into honors math, and now she's in study hall with me. But she's not so bad. Don't roll your eyes, Pri! HAHA. SO excited for our sleepover. 1 more day!

xoxo Cece

From: Vishal Gobin
To: Prianka Basak
Subject: Hi

Dear Prianka,

Sorry I didn't have time to answer your question at Bal Vihar. I am only here for the rest of this year probably. There is a trial program where they want to let kids take classes at both schools for middle and high school and I signed up to test it out. It's weird. The cafeteria hot dog was probably a bad choice.

Hope you are having a nice day.

Sincerely,
Vishal

Prianka, Cecily

PRIANKA

U think Gabs is acting weird?

CECILY

4 a sec I thought she was on this group text

Heart pounding 🤍🤍

PRIANKA

Would not be that stupid, thankyouverymuch 😒

So do u ⁉️ 😕

CECILY

Ummm

We need to stash phones the sec we hear her flush, k

17

We r texting behind her back @ a
sleepover

This is bad

PRIANKA

K

Answer me

CECILY

IDK

I feel bad talking bout her, even over text

PRIANKA

K

Sorry

Just worried

K she flushed

Put phone away

Dear Diary,

I couldn't write in you last night because I slept over at Cecily's house. It was fun but I felt like I had too many secrets. One, the Colin thing. Two, that we may be moving before the summer. They are my BFFs, but I couldn't bring it up. You are the only one who knows this stuff. I'm tired now. Bye.

Love,

Gabby

THE 🐶🐶🐶 MUSKETEERS

P C G

CECILY

Guys we need 2 decide what club 2 join this sem

🐶🐶🐶

GABRIELLE

Complicated bc I'm doing 1 night @ my dad's & 1 night @ my mom's now

Pickup times & buses & stuff . . . UGH

Maybe chorus?

Think they'll pick T-Swift songs?

CECILY

Prob

Mrs. Sempra likes to do current stuff

Ingrid always sang pop songs & stuff

Do it

GABRIELLE

K yeah

Fun 👏

PRIANKA

Now I wanna do chorus

Can we do more than 1 🙇

CECILY

Maybe, let's ask

We can all do chorus 2gether

That could be great 🎉 👯

GABRIELLE

We need a cool name tho

Like "Shake It Off Sisters" or something . . .

Ya know

Is there an emoji for 3 girls ⁉️

👯👯👯

PRIANKA

Yeah let's brainstorm

I gtg

Madre calling me 2 set table

Later, luvies! 💘

CECILY

Ciao 〰️

GABRIELLE

Bye bye mwah 😘 😘 😘

Cecily, Victoria

VICTORIA

🐶

CECILY

Who is this ⁉️⁉️

VICTORIA

Victoria

From homeroom

I was going over class list Ms. Enarack handed out & I saw ur # & figured I'd text

CECILY

Oh hi

Do u like dogs or something 🐩🐩

VICTORIA

yup luv them 🐾🐾🐾

Cool 👍 👍

VICTORIA

K um bye

FUN TO TEXT W/ U!!!!!!!!!! 😀 😄 😆 🙃

CECILY

K bye

THE GIRLS 🖤 🖤 🖤 🖤 🖤 🖤

P C G

CECILY

Guys, guess what happened when I was waiting for my mom 2 pick me up after Spanish extra help

GABRIELLE

??? 👂 👂

PRIANKA

Tell us

Y r u taking so long !!!!

CECILY

So u know how Ingrid said middle school valentine's dance is like major deal . . . 🩶

GABRIELLE

Yea GET TO THE POINT

CECILY

So Mrs. Lakely was leaving school & going 2 her car & she told me she's fac advisor 4 the dance again

& she remembered how Ingrid was such a huge help for it 2 years ago . . .

And she wants me 2 help organize a committee

!!!!!!!!!!!!!!!!

PRIANKA

R U SERIOUS RIGHT NOW ⁉️ 🫣 🫣

CECILY

YES YES YES YES

Pays to have a fab older sis 😎 😎

GABRIELLE

OMG! This means we can literally RUN the biggest event of our lives so far

Like we are in charge 👊🏻 👏🏻 👊🏻 👏🏻

CECILY

Haha yeah guess so

I mean we'll need 2 ask other people 2 join & stuff

Make posters & have a meeting

It can't just be us 3 👩 👩 👩

GABRIELLE

Right

PRIANKA

Soo cool

K gtg get ready 4 bed

C u at bus 1st thing in morn

Smooches 💋 💋

CECILY

MWAH 😍 😍 XOXO

GABRIELLE

XOXOXO 2 infinity 🐾 🤍 🖤 🐾 🤍 🖤

WE CRUSHED THAT
BADMINTON GAME!!!!!!!!!!! —Colin

I KNOW!!! GO TEAM Cs!!!! —Cecily

LUCKY 🐤🐤🐤

P C G

PRIANKA

We r luckiest peeps in the world

Did u see how long wait list was 4 chorus

How did we get so lucky 🎱 🍀 🎱 🍀

GABRIELLE

IHNC honestly 🙌 🙌 👏

CECILY

I know & Mrs. Sempra loved idea 4 our trio
4 solos & stuff

She was totes into it 😹😹😹😹😹

GABRIELLE

Rlly ❓

U saw her ‼️⁉️‼️

CECILY

She was subbing 4 homeroom today

I feel bad because new girl Victoria didn't get picked

She was sobbing 😿😭😢😿😭😢 in homeroom

GABRIELLE

Oh

She is my reading log buddy 📖📖

PRIANKA

Sad for Victoria 😢

CECILY

She says she really misses her friends at
her old school 😔 😫

PRIANKA

Oh sad 😥 😥

GABRIELLE

BTW when is 1st dance comm meeting
💃 💃 💃

CECILY

I need to finalize w/ Mrs. Lakely

Prob next week

Guys, Victoria asked for ur cell #s . . . 📱

GABRIELLE

Umm . . .

She already has mine from homeroom

PRIANKA

Yeah & I don't even know her 📵

30

CECILY

She's in our gym class right

GABRIELLE

Guys, can we get back 2 the dance comm disc?

CECILY

K let's make list of songs we may wanna do 4 chorus & then we can bring to Mrs. Sempra

& we can start practicing

GABRIELLE

K

Gonna go work on list & text 2 u guys

PRIANKA

Same ✓ ☑

From: Kimberly Higgins
To: Victoria Melford
Subject: I MISS YOU

Victoria,

I miss you so much. School isn't the same without your weird lunches and your crazy hairstyles. Are you still bringing cold eggplant pizza for lunch? What are your new friends like? Are the classes hard? We miss you so much. Write back ASAP.

Lots of love,
Kim

LUVIES

P   C   G

PRIANKA

Wait 1 q

This is 4 spring concert . . .

So we need cheery, summery songs?

CECILY

Yup I think so

PRIANKA

K

Cecily, Victoria

VICTORIA

Does this emoji girl look like me? 👧

CECILY

Ummm kinda

But u have brown hair

VICTORIA

I KNOW

CECILY

I gtg back 2 studying

C ya in homeroom 📖📕📗📕

VICTORIA

OK byeeeeeee 😝

Gabrielle, Victoria

VICTORIA

Hi! We can do reading log notes over text? 📚

GABRIELLE

I think it has to be like written on paper

Isn't that what Ms. Marburn said? 📝 📝

VICTORIA

IDK

Dear Diary,

I forgot to tell you there is a middle school dance!
And I am going to be on the planning committee!
I am so excited. I wonder if Colin will ask me to
dance. Or maybe I can ask him. I don't know how
any of that works. I wish I had an older sister to
ask. :(

Love,
Gabby

🎤🎤🎤 **GIRLZZZ**

GABRIELLE

ICB, M girls wanna b chorus trio 2! 🚫🚫

PRIANKA

I can

M girls always think they r stars of everything ⭐️ ✨ ⭐️ ⭐️ ✨ ⭐️

CECILY

Can I say that I don't think they r as bad as they used to b

They r in all my classes & they r actually kinda nice now.

PRIANKA

NO 🙈 🙈

GABRIELLE

NO U CANNOT 🆖 🆖

CECILY

Sheesh k

GABRIELLE

When did M girls become a thing n e way

I mean y r they even friends & popular & stuff 🐾 🐾

PRIANKA

Bc all their names start with M & they think they r cool 😝

CECILY

Maybe

PRIANKA

I can't figure it out 🤔

CECILY

Let's not waste time worrying about them & just be the awesomest peeps we can b 🐤🐤🐤

PRIANKA

Cece is a motivational speaker now! 📡📢

GABRIELLE

Hahahahahaah totes

PEEPSQUAD 🐤🐤🐤

CECILY

LOL LOL PEEPSQUAD gtg do hw 🐤🐤 🐣📚📚

LOL laterz

Bye 👋 👋 👋

COME AND JOIN THE PLANNING
COMMITTEE FOR THE MIDDLE SCHOOL
VALENTINE'S DAY DANCE!

Where: The Cafeteria
When: Thursday 1/15 After School
Who: HOPEFULLY YOU!

Questions: Email Cecily Anderson
candycorn413@gmail.com

READING LOG

Gabby—I feel the worst for Maddie, because she has to go along with Peggy . . . she wouldn't be this way on her own, ya know? Are you doing the Valentine's dance planning thing? I know this is just supposed to be for reading log notes, but I was curious. Let me know. —Victoria ♡♡♡

V—I know! I love Maddie! I think I am gonna go to the meeting. I'm not sure, though. OK, I am going to look over your reading log notes. You read fast! —Gabby

THE BEST SQUAD IN THE WORLD

PRIANKA

Did any1 eat that green bean salad @ lunch 2day? 🍴

CECILY

No . . . Y?

PRIANKA

Just checking

Stomach feels a bit off. 😵

GABRIELLE

Never eat anything green in school caf ⛔ 🚫 😨

PRIANKA

Why'd I never know that rule 😕 😫 😨

GABRIELLE

IHNC

Good luck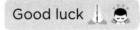

CECILY

Xoxo

BFFAEAEAEAEAEAEAEAEAE
😤😤😤😤😤😤

P C G

PRIANKA

What did I miss in school 2day

Doc doesn't think food poisoning from green bean salad fyi

CECILY

Phew

Umm u didn't miss much

No after-school chorus bc Mrs. Sempra out sick

Pos she ate green bean salad 2?

Need to investigate 👓 🧐 👓 🧐 👓

Peeps r signing up for dance comm 🙌 🙌 🙌 🙌

GABRIELLE

Who??

CECILY

Um well Keri Harvey & her BFFs + lot of girls IDK

Oh that kid Vishal sent me an email that he's comin

& Colin Hayes & Jared Remington r coming 2 👏 👏 🎉

PRIANKA

rlly?

PRIANKA

Gonna be big committee 👏 👏 🎉

CECILY

Yeah . . . Fun, right? ✌️

PRIANKA

Def! 👍

CECILY

I gtg help my mom fold laundry 👕 👕

Feel better, Pri 💨 😘

From: Victoria Melford
To: Kimberly Higgins, Nicole Landenor
Subject: Dance??

Do you guys have a Valentine's Day dance?
We have one here, and I am signing up to be
on the committee.

xo Victoria

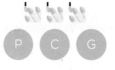

GABRIELLE

This is what my mom made for din

Barf

CECILY

What is that

(We had spaghetti)

GABRIELLE

Meat & tomato sauce? All mushy . . .

Like a taco w/o shell

Or a meatball but not a ball IDK

Crying 😂😂

PRIANKA

My stomach is still too iffy to see photo like that . . .

😷😷😷😷😷😷😷😷😷😷😷😷😷

Dear Diary,

Cecily just told us that Colin signed up for the dance committee. I AM FREAKING OUT. I am going to be so close to him, working on this, what if I forget how to talk? I NEED HELP. Should I tell my friends I like him?

Love,

Gabby

DANCE GIRLS 4EVA 🦢🦢🦢

P **C** **G**

CECILY

I know u guys will see email but 1st dance planning meeting is Thurs after school 🦢
🐥🦢🐥

GABRIELLE

😱🦢

CECILY

So excited!!!!!

Also M girls did not sign up

Said they r "too busy" 🐥 🐥

PRIANKA

Whatev

M girls prob think they r 2 cool for dance

So this is big

Need to plan my outfit & actually brush my hair that morn . . . 🙎🏻‍♀️

CECILY

Gonna be great but u guys need 2 bring ideas 2 meeting, k?

Like what we should do for theme & snacks & stuff 🎉 🎉 🎉 🍪 🍩 🍨

GABRIELLE

On it ☑️

CECILY

1 more thing

Victoria joined . . .

GABRIELLE

B

BLARGHEJKWJRKEJHWERHIUEWH1R!! 🐺 😫

CECILY

Don't be mean ☮️ ✌️

PRIANKA

She's really weird, Cece 🙅 🙅

CECILY

K but whatev

We can be nice to her

Bye bye, girls

Hw time 😘

GABRIELLE

ILYSM 🖤 🖤

Unknown, Gabrielle

MAYBE: COLIN

What pgs do we need 2 do for math ÷ — ➕✖ –Colin

GABRIELLE

How did u get my #

18-23, odd

COLIN

On class list Mr. Boskello passed around

My friends never write down the hw

Lost my planner thx

Cecily, Victoria

VICTORIA

Can't wait 2 talk bout dance!! 👯 🐧 👯

CECILY

Ya

VICTORIA

Do u want to start a group text so we can all discuss where we r going 4 dresses? 👗
👗👗👗

CECILY

Let's just talk at meeting, k?

VICTORIA

BUT WE NEED 2 SHOP 2GETHER!!!
👗👕👗👕

CECILY

I am really behind in math hw

Sorry, Victoria

C u tm

VICTORIA
U are always doing hw 📚📚📚📚

K

Prianka, Cecily

P C

PRIANKA
Cece, u there?

CECILY
Ya what's up?

Finishing sci lab

PRIANKA
I think Gabs really may be moving soon

It's happening 🏚️😫🏚️😩🏚️

Huh?

Y?

PRIANKA

We ran into her mom @ grocery store . . .

But I think there's a chance we can convince her Gabs needs 2 stay & finish the yr

CECILY

Ok . . . My throat hurts all of a sudden

What will we do w/o Gabs? & y hasn't she talked to us about it? 😾😩😢😾😩😢

PRIANKA

I dunno

We need her 2 stay 🙏💁

53

Let's talk tomrw after assembly

K nighty night 🌙🏙️🌉

Victoria wants us all 2 go shopping 2gether
4 the dance & text about it

NOOOOOO

Dear Diary,

Colin texted me about the math homework. I don't know what this means. I am going to save the text forever. He never, ever talks to me in person. But maybe he will now. Maybe we can just talk about math.

Love,
Gabby

Unknown, Prianka

NO CALLER ID

Buttcheeks

PRIANKA

??? Who is this???

NO CALLER ID
U have to guess

PRIANKA
Ummm Ingrid

NO CALLER ID
Who?

No, not Ingrid

PRIANKA
Kamal?

NO CALLER ID
No

PRIANKA
Ummm IHNC

NO CALLER ID
It's Vishal

PRIANKA
Oh um hi

Putting ur # in my fone so u can never do that again

Fine but I can always get new #

Not that easy

We'll see bout that . . .

Dear Gabby, I know we're only reading log partners but I don't understand why you and your friends never write back to my group texts. Did I do something wrong? Please explain. xoxo Victoria

Hi, Victoria,
You didn't do anything wrong. Sometimes we
forget to write back. —Gabby

Mom, Gabrielle

GABRIELLE

Mom, I am so mad at u

I refuse to talk to u in person

No way I am moving with u 2 Aspen

Yorkville is my home.

Will live here by myself if I have 2

I'll move in w/ Cecily or Prianka

Dear Gabrielle, I am willing to discuss this with you calmly, when you are ready. I love you. Mom

DANCE DANCE DANCE

👯 👯 👯 👯 👯 👯

(P) (C) (G) (V)

VICTORIA

Hiiiii, guys

Soooooooo excited 4 the dance

From: Vishal Gobin
To: Prianka Basak
Subject: COMPUTER LAB IS SO BORING

WHY IS THIS period so boring? All we do is practice typiNG. **DID YOU SIGN UP FOR THE BAL VIHAR** carnival? I am trying every font. Bye.

From: Prianka Basak
To: Vishal Gobin
Subject: DON'T GET ME IN TROUBLE

It's not boring. Don't get me in trouble. I love this font, though. Bye.

MEMO

From: Mr. Carransey, Principal, Yorkville Middle School
To: ALL SIXTH-GRADE PARENTS
Re: Cell phone use in school

I hope the New Year is off to a good start for everyone.

I wanted to remind all of you that phones are not to be used during the school day unless directed by a teacher for an actual assignment.

Also, I encourage you all to speak to your children about social media, who they're texting, and what is taking place in these text conversations. We must open the lines of communication between parents and students when it comes to our ever-changing world of technology. I appreciate your attention to this matter.

Sincerely,
Edward Carransey
Principal
Yorkville Middle School

Be the change you want to see in the world.—Gandhi

BFFFFFFFF

GABRIELLE

Where r u guys?

I'm 1st 1 here 😨 😪 😬

CECILY

Coming

Had to pee

PRIANKA

EWWW

I'm so nervous

😥 😵 😥

Hiding in band room 2 get ready 🎵 🎵 🎼

Cecily, Victoria

VICTORIA

R u there?

CECILY

👆

VICTORIA

Heard u & ur friends talking at the end of the meeting about stuff 4 the dance & I felt really left out 💔 💔

CECILY

Oh so sorry - don't feel left out

We r all on the committee & we can all discuss 👭👬👭

VICTORIA

I know, but u guys r all so close & I want 2 set up a time 4 us all 2 hang

U never wb 2 my group texts 😒 😫

Isn't this baby angel so cute? 👼

CECILY

Yeah cute

What about this cat 🐱

VICTORIA

EVEN CUTER. ✔✔

From: Victoria Melford
To: Kimberly Higgins, Nicole Landenor
Subject: THIS SCHOOL IS CRAZY

Hi, guys—

I hate this school. I went to the dance committee meeting and no one talked to me! I text people and they don't write back! What is going on? I was cool at Bayberry, wasn't I? I mean, not cool cool but, like, normal cool? I feel like everything is backwards here.

I'm in study hall now. So boring. How can I convince my mom to move back?

SMOOCHES! Victoria

THE GIRLZZZZZ

P   C   G

GABRIELLE

So that was chaotic

CECILY

IK

We'll never agree 2 a theme

& it's like 5 weeks away!!

Also, Victoria really wants 2 hang out w/ us. She keeps asking

I think we should just do it 2 be nice ☮️ ✌️

PRIANKA

K I don't think we r being mean to Victoria

But we don't have to hang out w/ her

Also we'll agree on theme

We may just have 2 have anonymous voting or something

Did u c how mad Marissa got when I suggested NYC as the theme

She was like furious 😔 🥊 😠 😣 😏

CECILY

I guess bc she used to live there when she was like 5, and feels angry she had 2 move 😠 😠 😠

PRIANKA

Maybe but come on - that mad? Ew 🙄

GABRIELLE

All the boys cared about was food.

Did u notice that?

PRIANKA

Boys always care about food 🍟 🍕 🍪 🍩 🍄

GABRIELLE

Yeah true

PRIANKA

I gtg we have 1st chorus rehearsal tomrw

Don't forget 💚 🎶 💚

GABRIELLE

ILYSM, girlies. 🌷 💚 🌍

CECILY

Smooch 😽 😘 😽

PRIANKA

Xoxooxxo

Cecily, Mara

MARA

Cecily, is this your #?

CECILY

Yes hi 🤚🤚🤚🤚🤚🤚🤚

MARA

Hi! Hope it's not weird that I'm texting u

But since u gave out ur number 2 the dance committee . . .

At 1st I didn't want to join but now I do really want to help w/ dance. 💃💃💃

CECILY

It's not weird

Also u could just ring my bell

Did u forget u live next door? LOL 🏠🏠

MARA

HAHA. DUH! OK!

Well see u tomrw!

THE GIRLZZZZZ

P C G

CECILY

Guys, Mara just texted me out of the blue, saying she really does want 2 help with the dance.

PRIANKA

STOP

WHAT???!!! ⬤⬤ 🔋

GABRIELLE

Y?!?!?

CECILY

No idea.

GABRIELLE

Cece is gonna become M girl 👧👧

CECILY

Um no

I will not ✋🖐️

PRIANKA

K . . .

VICTORIA

Hi, Prianka, Gabrielle & Cecily

HIIII!

So excited we can all group text 👯👯👯👯

👯👯👯👯👯👯👯

P   C   G

PRIANKA

HELLO? ANY1 THERE?

R we all ignoring Victoria?

WHAT IS GOING ON?

Also, u r never gonna believe this

CECILY

What ⁉❓⁉❓

GABRIELLE

Sorry, I am behind. What's going on?

PRIANKA

Vishal is having a boy-girl bday party!

OUR 1st EVER!!!! 👫👫👫

CECILY

OMG

GABRIELLE

When ❓❓❓

Where ❓❓❓

Are we invited???

TELL ALL NOW ‼️‼️

PRIANKA

K IDK if we r all invited

I know I am invited . . . Invites are 📫📪📫

He's like having a real deal 12th birthday

Who does that

CECILY

I guess Vishal 😂 😂

PRIANKA

Haha

Right

Pos bc he changed schools & needs to b social

CECILY

It's gonna be awesome

But better if we r there obv 👍 👍 👍

GABRIELLE

Think M girls will be invited?

PRIANKA

I think they will . . .

Did u know Marissa has been talking to Vishal after study hall?

I try to ignore it but it's happening

I mean their dads know each other from college or something, so it's not THAT crazy

But it's still crazy 😫 😫 😫 😫

CECILY

Wait - how do u know about the party

Did u already get the invite

Eavesdropping again? Hee hee

😆 😆 😆

PRIANKA

I had to hear from MY MOM

SO LAME.

GABRIELLE

No offense but that is lame-o 2 the extreme

CECILY

Gabs come on

Not the nicest response

☮ ☮ ☮ ☮ ☮ ☮ ☮ ☮

GABRIELLE

Fine sorry

But we need 2 step up our game

If parties r happening we need 2 b the ones
2 find out about them

Ya know 😼 😼 😼

PRIANKA

K, Gabs . . . U lead the way.

Bc u know about soooo many parties 🙄

CECILY

Guys, stop fighting

Remember we promised we wouldn't fight over text

☮☮☮☮☮☮☮☮☮☮☮☮☮

PRIANKA

Ummm 🤔

CECILY

Yes, u do remember

GABRIELLE

Fine

Sorry, I'm just in bad mood 😒

PRIANKA

Y

GABRIELLE

My mom is still talking about moving 🚚🏠

PRIANKA

K we will make sure you don't move but 1st thing is getting invited 2 the party

So let's meet @ lockers first thing tomw morn & figure out what we r going 2 do 2 get invites

CECILY

K MWAH

GABRIELLE

Xoxo

PARTY PARTY PARTY PARTY
PARTY PARTY

Where: Casa de Gobin
(Vishal's pad)
16 Piedmont Drive

When: February 2, 6pm

Why: Last-minute party because
VISHAL IS TURNING 12, YO!

RSVP: VGobs1342@gmail.com

Prianka, Cecily

P C

CECILY

Pri we need 2 come up with game plan 2
make sure Gabs doesn't move

Like we do 1 thing each day 2 convince her mom 2 stay

🙇🔆🙇🔆🙇🔆🙇🔆🙇🔆🙇🔆🙇

PRIANKA

Ummm I like it

But what can we do 🤔

CECILY

Leave note in her mailbox every day with diff reason of y Yorkville is best place 2 live
😀😀😀😀📬📪📫📪

PRIANKA

K!

Or email if we can't make it over there . . .
📧💻📧💻📧

CECILY

Good backup plan 👏👏✔✔

PRIANKA

Fab 👏👏👏👏🎉🎉🎉🎉

👧👧👧👧
P C G V

VICTORIA

IS ANY1 OUT THERE???? HELLOOOOOO
I'VE TEXTED U GUYS SO MANY TIMES &
NO 1 RESPONDS!!!!!!!! 🙌🙌🙌🙌 🐱

DID EVERY1 GET INVITED 2 VISHAL'S
PARTY!? Sorry 4 all caps ⚒️⚒️⚒️⚒️⚒️
⚒️⚒️⚒️

From: Victoria Melford
To: Vishal Gobin
Subject: PARTY!!!!!!!!!!!!!!!!!!!!!!!!!!!!!!!

Hi, Vishal,

I heard you are having a party. We just moved here and my address isn't in the school directory.

I would love to come to your party.

See you in Global Studies!

Victoria

SICK CECE 😟 😟 😟

P C G

CECILY

I don't think u guys r going to see this until way l8r

I'm home puking my guts out 🤮

Some1 needs 2 respond 2 Victoria's group text

PLZZZZZZ 😩 😫 😩 😩 ⬇ ⬇

SICK CECE 😟 😟 😟

P C G

CECILY

Still here

On a puke break

BUT GUESS WHO GOT INVITED TO
VISHAL'S PARTY

Obvs u will b 2 . . . 👏👏

THE CREW 👊👊👊

PRIANKA

Ok, so we r all invited

YAY

Cece, how r u feeling 🙁

CECILY

BLARGHSJWKJNDKJSH 🤢🥴

GABRIELLE

Wow, that bad huh? 🙀😪😢

CECILY

I may not be back tomw 🙀 . . . & we have dance comm

U guys gotta take over for me, k?

GABRIELLE

Um

I'll try . . .

PRIANKA

We can do this

& YAY TO THIS PARTY

K - we have 2 plan outfits 👗👠👢👔👖

CECILY

Gtg . . . Sick Cece over here 😷😴😷😷

PRIANKA

FEEL BETTER 💕💞🤍

GABRIELLE

Feel better, Cece. 🤍🤍🤍

THE CREW 👊 👊 👊

(P) (C) (G)

CECILY

Um so don't freak out but Mara texted me to see how I'm feeling . . .

Guys, I feel like M girls want 2 be friends w/ us

They r honestly nice I promise 🐧 🐧 🐧 🐧 🐧 🐧

GABRIELLE

WHOA

K but u DEK what happened @ lunch 2day!!

CECILY

???

PRIANKA

⁉️⁉️

GABRIELLE

K so there was def a fight b/t M girls

Mara got mad at Marissa saying she was talking 2 Mae behind her back

😨 😨 😨 😨 😨 😨

PRIANKA

HA - this sounds crazy 👂 👂

GABRIELLE

It was

Mrs. Manuso had 2 get involved

& u know that's bad . . . 😈 😈 😈

CECILY

So what happened

?????

GABRIELLE

All 3 of them were crying . . . 😿 😿 😿

> Then Mara stopped me on the way 2 math
> 2 ask me where u were, Cece

CECILY

What? Really?

GABRIELLE

Yup

> I think she's trying 2 break away from them 😣😣

CECILY

No way

M girls are tight as can be 👀

GABRIELLE

I know

Soooooo weird right

CECILY

Well, Mara is the nicest . . .

PRIANKA

Just stay away from Marissa 👟👟

She's the 1 who is in 🤍 w/ Vishal 👫

GABRIELLE

K whatev

My mom calling me

GTG 👣

PRIANKA

BYE 🖐️

CECILY

Hope 2 be back in school tomw

ILY 💜💜💜💜💜💜

From: Priscilla Melford
To: Edward Carransey
Subject: Victoria Melford experiencing social cruelty

Dear Mr. Carransey:

My daughter, Victoria (sixth grade), is being excluded at every turn. She is new to the school. As you know, we had to move midyear. Victoria joined the dance committee to meet new friends, but they do not include her in plans outside of school, despite many attempts. She is consistently left out of group texting communication. It is affecting her schoolwork and she is experiencing immense anxiety.

Also, it seems the students are overly concerned about dates for the Valentine's Day dance. This is not appropriate. I do not feel that dates should be allowed for a sixth-grade dance.

I would like to set a meeting with you to

discuss what can be done about these two issues.

Sincerely,
Priscilla Melford

Live, laugh, love.

Reason #1 why
you need to stay in
Yorkville:
The best friends in
the world.
♡ xoxo

Unknown, Prianka

NO CALLER ID

Hello Prianka

BARF BRAIN!!!!!!!!

PRIANKA

??? Who r u?

🧹🧹🧹 CREW

P   C   G

PRIANKA

Any1 else get BARF BRAIN text?

CECILY

No . . . But stomach bug going around obv
😵😫

I didn't

PRIANKA

GUYS, this is serious

Mystery texter

PLEASE HELP

Remember what Mr. Carransey said about social cruelty

CECILY

Ask who it is!

PRIANKA

I DID

BFFFFFFFF

(P) (C) (G)

GABRIELLE

Nice note in my mailbox, Pri 📬 📪

PRIANKA

HUH⁉️

GABRIELLE

I know ur handwriting, silly!

My mom thought it was sweet

PRIANKA

So did it work 😼 😆

GABRIELLE

IDK but thanx 🕯️ 👸 🕯️ 👸 🕯️

Unknown, Prianka

NO CALLER ID
BARF BRAIN

PRIANKA
WHO IS THIS??!!

ANSWER ME

I AM GOING 2 CALL THE POLICE 🚓🚔🚨👮

NO CALLER ID
Calm down

PRIANKA
TELL ME

NO CALLER ID
Ok, it's Vishal

Vishal, Prianka

VISHAL

Sorry

PRIANKA

Huh . . . Y did u just text me BARF BRAIN

VISHAL

My brother did 👻 👽 🤖 👻 💀 👺 👹 😈 😈 from his phone

HAHAHAAHAHAAHAHA

SoRrY

I was using his phone & then he stole it

TOLD U I COULD FIND OTHER NUMBERS

HAHAHAHA

PRIANKA

Bye

PRIANKA

It was Vishal's brother . . . WEIRD

CECILY

That is weird 😦

GABRIELLE

GUYS, u r never going 2 believe this

Ya know how Mrs. Hughes lives next door & my mom and her exercise 2gether sometimes

CECILY

Yeah?

GABRIELLE

Wellllllllll, some of the moms called school & complained that our grade is getting too crazy with dates & stuff 4 the dance & they may not even allow dates AT ALL 🐻 🐻 🐻

PRIANKA

What!!!!!! That is crazy!!!!!!!!

Cece, did Ingrid's grade have dates?

CECILY

Umm . . . I think so.

GABRIELLE

Who do u think complained?

CECILY

No idea!!!

PRIANKA

This is crazy 😔 😔

Did u guys tell ur moms we were going to ask boys to the dance

I didn't

MINE would FLIP!

🐫

CECILY

I didn't . . . IDC if I bring a date

Do u guys?

I just wanna have fun with every1 👯‍♀️👭🧜‍♀️

GABRIELLE

IDK how to ask some1 2 be my date!!!

My mom would prob freak & then try to make us move even more 🚫➖🚫➖

CECILY

We need 2 get 2 the bottom of this

But here's the thing - peeps don't all have 2 do the same thing

If some1 wants 2 bring a date, fine

If not, also fine

Ya know?

Every1 is going CRAZY. ✋ ☮ ✋ ☮ ✋ ☮

PRIANKA

I KNOW

WIGO?!?

madness 😐 😐 😐

CECILY

OK

KEEP CALM, PEOPLE, KEEP CALM

Going to bed now XOX

PRIANKA

Night night 🤍 🤍

GABRIELLE

MWAH 🤍 💋 🤍 💋 🤍 💋

From: Priscilla Melford
To: Sixth-Grade Parents Association
Subject: Valentine's Day Dance

Dear fellow parents:

It has come to my attention that some of the students are trying to bring dates to the Valentine's Day dance. I do not feel this is appropriate, and I think the administration needs to get involved.

Please add this to the agenda for the PA meeting on Thursday.

Sincerely,
Priscilla Melford

Live, laugh, love.

Dear Diary,

Colin talked to me in math today. He asked when the quiz was. He also asked me if I am going to Vishal's party. I am freaking out. I have to tell my friends I like him, but I am so scared because what if he doesn't like me? I don't know what to do.

Love,
Gabby

Prianka, Cecily

PRIANKA

Cece, u there? 🩶

CECILY

Doing sci lab

Wuz ⬆️?

PRIANKA

Have u left any more notes

CECILY

Yea but we need 2 keep doing it

My mom had dinner w/ Gabby's mom 2night & I think she really wants 2 move 😢😫🙀

PRIANKA

NOOOO 😫😫

We will keep working on it

Gtg do this lab

Don't be mad, but Mara is coming over after school again tomw

She asked me to hang out

K, promise? Don't be mad 🕯️ 🙇

PRIANKA

Calm down

Weren't u the 1 who said to stay calm

I'm not mad ✌️

CECILY

OK

XOXOX 💔 ❤️

PRIANKA

Xo

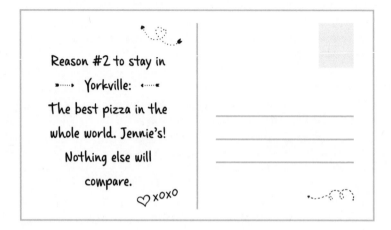

Reason #2 to stay in
Yorkville:
The best pizza in the
whole world. Jennie's!
Nothing else will
compare.

♡ xoxo

From: Colin Hayes
To: Cecily Anderson
Subject: BEST BADMINTON PARTNERS EVER

Yo. I am in study hall and had an idea. What if we suggested to Mr. Peeds and the gym department that we start a badminton team? We are so good! I think kids would be into it. And maybe that would help fulfill my community service requirement?

Probably not. HAHAHA.
Peace out,
Colin

Prianka, Gabrielle

PRIANKA

Hi, Gabs 🤍

GABRIELLE

Hiiiiii

PRIANKA

I think we need emergency sleepover this weekend

Cece is hanging out w/ Mara after school again tomw

Don't tell her I told u

Maybe Cece does want to be friends w/ them . . . & she's trying to break away from us 🙄

And Victoria is trying to hijack us

Don't want 2 be mean 2 her but she is sooooo annoying

GABRIELLE

Ok this is a big deal!!!!!!!!!! 😰 😨 😰 😨 😰

PRIANKA

IK

WE NEED TO FIX THIS! 👍👍

From: Darlene Lakely
To: Cecily Anderson
Subject: Valentine's Day Dance Logistics

Hi, Cecily,

I wondered if you could meet five to ten minutes before lunch on Wednesday so we can discuss some logistics about the dance.

Thank you,
Mrs. Lakely

Mara, Cecily

M   C

MARA
Was so much fun 2 hang w/ u 😊 😊

CECILY
👀 had fun 2!! 👏 👏

MARA

Good luck w/ Mrs. Lakely meeting

I'm sure it is nothing major 🙏

CECILY

Fingers crossed

Also Colin Hayes wants 2 start a badminton team

So funny, right? 😂 😂

MARA

THAT WOULD BE SO FUNNY

LMK what happens w/ Lakely 🩶 🩶

EMERGENCY SLEEPOVER

!! 🛏 !!

(P) (C) (G)

Sleepover sat?

PRIANKA

👍

CECILY

👏 👏

From: Cecily Anderson
To: Colin Hayes
Subject: Badminton Team

I like your idea. Just so busy now with the dance stuff. But maybe we can do it closer to the spring.

Victoria, Cecily

VICTORIA

Still didn't get invite 2 Vishal's party

I emailed him & he didn't wb

What should I do???? 😔 🥺 😫 🥺

● ● ●

CECILY

Sometimes 📪 📫 is weird

Don't worry

VICTORIA

I AM SO STRESSED

Also ur friends don't respond 2 my group texts

What is wrong w/ me?? 😈 👿

Phone dying

Let's talk tomrw

 **U**

P   C   G

CECILY

U guys, this Victoria thing is making me crazy

She's really hurt

We need 2 respond or just be nice or something

IDK!!!!! 🕯️ ☮️ ✌️

PRIANKA

But IDK her!!!! 😐 😕 😐

GABRIELLE

😫 😫 😫 SAME

TBH I feel bad but we don't have any classes 2gether besides gym + Eng

She asked 2 switch & be my badminton partner but Mr. Peeds said no

I am stuck w/ Becky Willard

She's so much better than I am & I think she hates me

Also, I am already so stressed with hw

CECILY

OK

Let's talk about it @ sleepover 🐩 🐩

READING LOG

It's been nice having a break from reading log, hasn't it? Here are my pages. Can we hang out sometime? —Victoria ♡♡♡

I kind of missed reading log, to be honest. I'm really stressed because we may be moving. I feel like Wanda! :(:(:(I'll let u know when I am free to hang. —Gabby

Cecily, Mara

C M

CECILY

So the Mrs. Lakely meeting wasn't that crazy but she is concerned about dates thing

She wanted to know what I thought about it

MARA

What do u think ??

CECILY

IDK

People r getting kinda crazy.

& some peeps might not have a date . . . 😪 😢

MARA

Yeah. Hmmm . . .

Well, we still have time

I gtg finish English essay

C u tomw 💕

CECILY

Bye bye

From: Beverly Flam
To: Priscilla Melford
Subject: Meeting to discuss Victoria

Dear Mrs. Melford:

I wanted to set up a time to meet in person to discuss how Victoria is adjusting to her new school. Please get back to me at your earliest convenience.

Kind regards,
Beverly Flam

Peace. It does not mean to be in a place where there is no noise, trouble, or hard work. It means to be in the midst of those things and still be calm in your heart.
—Unknown

Vishal, Prianka

VISHAL

What do u think peeps should do at my party

PRIANKA

Ummmm

VISHAL

Snacks + video games 🎮 🎮

PRIANKA

I never knew there was a video game emoji! COOL!

VISHAL

So?

PRIANKA

Will try and think of ideas 💡 💡

From: Kimberly Higgins
To: Victoria Melford
Subject: GUESS WHAT?

V-girl:

My phone got taken away bc I got a C in math. But I can still email. LOL!

Guess who asked about you today? Mark Carlyle! Remember him? He was like "I haven't seen Victoria around." And I was like "That's because she moved!"

LOL LOL LOL
LOVE YOU TONS!
K-girl

Mom, Prianka

MOM

Prianka, get downstairs this instant. Texting seems to be the only way to reach you these days, which is very disappointing. Love, Mom

PRIANKA

???

MOM

Get down here now. Your teacher called and I am very disappointed.

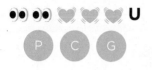

PRIANKA

OMG OMG OMG OMG OMG OMG

CECILY

??????

GABRIELLE

Wuzzzzz ⬆️ ⬆️

PRIANKA

Ms. Peabody called my mom bc Victoria said I am being so mean to her

& my mom said if I don't stop I can't go to Vishal's party or 2 the dance

BUT IT ISN'T EVEN TRUE!!!!!!!!! 😳😩🙀😳😩🙀😳😩🙀😳😩🙀

CECILY

WOW

OMG

😧 😧 😵 😠

I KNOW

I don't get this

R we all gonna get calls home!?!?!?
😼 😼 😼

PRIANKA

IDK 😫

MEMO

From: Mr. Carransey, Principal, Yorkville Middle School
To: ALL SIXTH-GRADE STUDENTS

Reminder that we have an assembly immediately following fifth period TODAY. Please meet in the auditorium. Thank you.

Sincerely,
Edward Carransey
Principal
Yorkville Middle School

Be the change you want to see in the world. —Gandhi

Vishal, Prianka

VISHAL

Who is Victoria

I'm confused

She emailed me

PRIANKA

She came from Philly

She's in comp lab with me but IDK her that well

VISHAL

OK

From: Priscilla Melford
To: Aarushi Gobin
Subject: Our children

Dear Aarushi:

We haven't met as of yet but we have a mutual friend—Joy Greely—and she speaks very highly of you. I wanted to get in touch regarding your son Vishal's party. I want my daughter, Victoria, to handle her personal matters on her own, so I instructed her to email Vishal, but she has not heard back. She will be very disappointed if she is not invited to his party. I wondered if an exception could be made just this once, as she is still adjusting to a new school.

Thank you,
Priscilla

Live, laugh, love.

 **SQUADDDDD**

P C G

PRIANKA

Soooooo . . . Victoria's mom got my mom's # & now my mom said that if I don't let her come 2 Vishal's party with us then I can't go. 😭😭

GABRIELLE

WHAT ⁉️⁉️⁉️⁉️

PRIANKA

I KNOW

How did this even happen

CECILY

Guys, it'll be ok

We can all meet @ ice cream place before

Isn't that a block away from where Vishal lives

PRIANKA

I guess

I mean, my mom did say she doesn't think
we r being mean but that V's mom really
wants her 2 have friends & she's having
hard time @ new school

CECILY

So it'll be fine

HONESTLY

Better to just be nice ☮️ ✌️

GABRIELLE

FINE

PARTY PEOPLE 🎉🎉🎉🎉🎉

P C G V

VICTORIA

OMG U GUYS!!!

SO excited 4 Vishal's party & 2 go 2gether!!!!

CECILY

Yay!

GABRIELLE

👍

PRIANKA

👍

THE REAL 🐦 SQUAD

(P) (C) (G)

GABRIELLE

But does she have to hang out w/ us the whole time??

PRIANKA

Wait, did u just respond to our group text w/ Victoria w/ that????

GABRIELLE

No

I'm not that dumb

😬 😬 😬 😬

PRIANKA

PHEW

CECILY

STAY CALM, PEOPLE

✌️ ✌️ ✌️ ✌️ ✌️

From: Nicole Landenor
To: Victoria Melford
Subject: HAVE SO MUCH FUN!!!!!

I'm in English now and supposed to be writing an essay and I miss you soooooo much!

Kim told me you're going to a boy-girl party. OMG, have so much fun! I want all details after. Did I tell you that Robbie Shenz likes me? I think I like him, too. Okay, bye.

Hugs,
Nic

Unknown, Victoria

NO CALLER ID

Y R U @ this party

?? Who is this

NO CALLER ID

U R not friends w/ any1 here

Mara, Cecily

M C

MARA

I am missing Vishal's party bc I finally got stomach flu every1 had 🤢 🤮 🤧 😩 🤮 🤧 🤮 🤮 😷 🤮

CECILY

Oh no!

Will miss u 🤮 🤧 🤮

MARA

Thanks, have fun

If I'm better tomw let's discuss the dance

I have ideas

CECILY
CECILY

K, feel better 💕 🖤

Prianka, Cecily

P C

PRIANKA

Where r M girls?

Weird I am texting u when u r right here, but I didn't want anyone 2 overhear

👧 👧

CECILY

Hee hee

Mara is sick 😵 😫

PRIANKA

K

So I guess the other 2 decided to stay home?

Gabs has been sitting next to Colin 4 like hours now . . . 😮😮😮😮😜

CECILY

I guess so . . .

Where is Victoria?

PRIANKA

IDK

This party is weird

Vishal texts me all the time but ignoring me here & all he's doing is 🎮 🎮 w/ Jared & those boys

CECILY

Weird party

Let's go soon, k? 🕯

PRIANKA

K

ILY

Unknown, Victoria

? V

NO CALLER ID

U don't look like U R having fun

Y R U here 👽 👾 😈 😠 👹 👺 💀 👻 👽

VICTORIA

I'm leaving this lame party & I'm telling Mr.
Carransey about these texts

VICNICKIM ◆ ◆ ◆

VICTORIA

U guys, this party is terrible

I hate it

I am getting rude anonymous mystery texts

NICOLE

Really ⁉️ 😩 🐱 😲

KIMBERLY

Ewww 👎 👎

VICTORIA

Wish I was w/ u guys now 😿 😿

PARTY PEOPLE 🎉 🎉 🎉 🎉 🎉

VICTORIA

My mom is coming to pick me up

IDK where u guys r!

BFFAEAEAEAEAE 😩 😩 😩 😩

CECILY

K, so that was def craziest party in history

PRIANKA

So glad it's over

Vishal ignored me

I AM SO MAD 😠 😠 😡 😠

Colin talked to me about sports and stuff I didn't care about 😒 😒 😒 😒

I just sat there

CECILY

Phone battery died so I never got that text from Victoria & I didn't even see her leave!

PRIANKA

I didn't see her either & when I took my jacket off

I left 📱 in pocket!

GABRIELLE

Weird we haven't heard from her since party 😬 😬 😬 😬

PRIANKA

IDK

CECILY

??

MEMO

From: Mr. Carransey, Principal, Yorkville Middle School
To: ALL SIXTH-GRADE PARENTS
Re: Ongoing Social Cruelty

Dear parents:

The cruelty via text message and other electronic communication continues in the sixth-grade class. We must work together to eradicate this problem. I am calling an emergency meeting of administrators, teachers, and parents Thursday evening at 7:00 p.m. I expect to see everyone there. If we cannot solve this very serious problem, the annual Valentine's Day dance will be canceled.

Thank you for your attention to this matter.

Edward Carransey
Principal
Yorkville Middle School

Be the change you want to see in the world.—Gandhi

dear colin,

I know it's weird to write a note like this, but I just need to tell you that you're so cute. you're the cutest boy in the whole grade, and I don't think you even know it.

—your secret admirer ♡ ♡ ♡

DA CREW

P C G

PRIANKA

Did ur parents tell u what happened @ the meeting? 😲 😲

GABRIELLE

!??

PRIANKA

There's an app parents can get where they can SEE our phones

Like from their phones . . . 📱➡️📱➡️📱➡️📱

CECILY

Uhh. Do u guys have lots of secrets? 😂 😂

PRIANKA

No . . .

GABRIELLE

Noo . . .

CECILY

Guys, they'll prob look once & then get bored

Let's just be extra boring the next few days. 😂 😂

PRIANKA

YES. Thank u, genius Cece. 👍 👍

GABRIELLE

But we are 2 cool 2 be boring. 😉 👩

CECILY

1 other thing

We gotta be super nice to Victoria

Dance will be canceled if parents keep complaining ☮ ✌🏻

PRIANKA

But it's not only us!

& we r not even mean

😡 😡 😡

GABRIELLE

I'm nice 2 her

CECILY

K so group text with VM starts tomorrow

Haha her initials r VM like voicemail . . .
😂 😂

GABRIELLE

But we can't be like over the top nicey

I mean, ya know . . .

PRIANKA

K, whatev it takes

CECILY

LOL

GABRIELLE

Mwah

Bye

See you tomw 💜 💜 💜

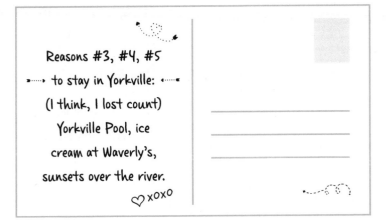

Reasons #3, #4, #5
⬤⬤⬤→ to stay in Yorkville: ←⬤⬤⬤
(I think, I lost count)
Yorkville Pool, ice
cream at Waverly's,
sunsets over the river.
♡ xoxo

Colin, Gabrielle

COLIN

Yo I found a super weird secret note in my locker

GABRIELLE

Wha??

COLIN

IDK

Like secret admirer or something

GABRIELLE

Really? Weird!!

COLIN

Do u know anyone who likes me

GABRIELLE

Uhhh . . . IHNC

COLIN

Ok, well, if u find out let me know

GABRIELLE

K

Dear Diary,

I did something crazy and left a note in Colin's locker and now I am totally regretting it. Why did I do it? I don't know. He talked to me at the party and I just had to do something. ACK. This is hell.

Love,
Gabby

From: Colin Hayes
To: Cecily Anderson
Subject: Note

Yo badminton partner—I got a secret admirer note. Do you know who it could be?

From: Diana Katz
To: Manjula Basak, Elizabeth Anderson
Subject: App?

Hi, ladies,

Did you download this app? It seems so confusing. I did something terrible and snooped in G's diary, and it's all about some boy, Colin? What is happening? We need dinner ASAP to figure these girls out. Ahhh—remember when they were babies? The good old days. Now diapers and colic and naps seem easy . . .

xoxo Diana

BABEZZZ

PRIANKA

Ladies . . .

CECILY

Hey wut ⬆️?

PRIANKA

I'm gonna start group text with VM, k?

CECILY

U guys hear about secret note in Colin's locker

GABRIELLE

I guess he has a secret admirer

?⬇️?

Whatevs 🤍🤍

PRIANKA

Bet it's 1 of M girls

Cece, u gotta find out from Mara

CECILY

U think?

They don't even rlly know Colin

GABRIELLE

He's obvi cutest kid in the grade . . . 😬😐😐😎

PRIANKA

He is??? 😂 😂

GABRIELLE

IDK

CECILY

K

Just start group chat w/ V 👍

From: Cecily Anderson
To: Colin Hayes
Subject: RE: Note

Hi, Badminton Partner—

No idea who sent you the note! Mysterious . . .

GIRLIESSSSS

P C G V

PRIANKA

Just wanted to say hey 👋

CECILY

HEY HEY! 👋

GABRIELLE

Hiiiii 👋

PRIANKA

Victoria, r u there?

VICTORIA

Hi!

PRIANKA

Soo what's going on???

VICTORIA

Nada

 **BFFs**

P   C   G

PRIANKA

Guys, there is nothing to text w/ her about . . .

CECILY

U r going 2 get confused about which text u r on & say something by mistake

PRIANKA

No

I won't

It's ok 👍👍

I'll ask if she knows about the colin note 😱

GIRLIESSSSS 🙋🙋🙋🙋

P C G V

GABRIELLE
Do u guys have any idea who sent colin that note

😬 😬 😬 😬 😬

PRIANKA
NOPE

CECILY
Me neither

So weird 😎😎

VICTORIA

I heard about this in math

So weird

He's like super serious about finding out who sent it

GABRIELLE

So crazy

V, who do u think it is

VICTORIA

IDK

Maybe Kelly O'Neal 👧

GABRIELLE

WHAT ‼️

No way 🚫 ➖ 🙈 🙉 🙊

VICTORIA

IDK

I just said maybe . . . 😣 😣

🐤 🐤 🐤 BFFs

P C G

PRIANKA

She has no idea what she is talking about

⊖

CECILY

Pri, stop doing side chats ⊖ 🚫

GABRIELLE

Kelly O'Neal does not like Colin

That's like, craziness . . .

I don't think she likes any1

She doesn't even really talk 😣 😣

PRIANKA

I KNOW

CECILY

Guys, u r being really mean

Aren't our moms looking at our phones w/ that app

WIGO 🚇🚇🚇

PRIANKA

UGH this feels so stressful 😡 😡 😡 😡

GIRLIESSSSS 💅 💅 💅

P   C   G   V

PRIANKA

I don't think Kelly O'Neal knows who Colin is

🙈 🙊 🙈

VICTORIA

They sit next to each other in Spanish 👫👫👫

PRIANKA

Oh

CECILY

So what else is going on 🎵🎵🎵

GABRIELLE

Nada

So much math hw

Cryinnggggggggg

📚📚📚📚

VICTORIA

I knowwwwwwwwwwwwwwwwwwwwwww

PRIANKA

Uhhh, Victoria is SO annoying guys

Please

Can this end? 🙏 😤 🙏 😤

VICTORIA

???

 **BFFs**

P   C   G

CECILY

PRIANKA ASHWINI BASAK

DO U SEE WHAT U JUST DID???

😠 😠 😠 😠

PRIANKA

😥

OMG I thought that was other group text

I feel soooooo bad

GABRIELLE

OMG what r we going to do 😱 😱

CECILY

We aren't gonna do anything, gabs

Pri has to figure this out

I gtg

GABRIELLE

Uhhh ok

Oops, good luck, Pri

GIRLIESSSSS 🐾🐾🐾

(P) (C) (G) (V)

PRIANKA

I'm so sorry Victoria

My bro was annoying me & I got confused & meant to send that about my bro . . .

I typed ur name by mistake 🐺🐺🐺

VICTORIA

Ok yeah right

I gtg

💔💔

PRIANKA

SO SORRY

💔💔💔💔💔💔💔💔💔💔💔💔💔💔💔
💔💔💔

Colin, Gabrielle

COLIN

Soooo . . . Did u find anything out about who wrote that letter?

GABRIELLE

No

IHNC

Y r u asking me

COLIN

Bc u know stuff, Gabs . . .

I need ur help

ILY2SM

GABRIELLE

Guys, I have to tell u something . . .

CECILY

??

GABRIELLE

K, so . . . Ready?

CECILY

Ready go puhlease !!!!

GABRIELLE

K, so I was the 1 who sent anon note to Colin bc I've liked him 4 so long & I'm sorry I never told u guys but I was so embarrassed

He keeps texting me to see if I know who sent it

GABRIELLE

HE CALLED ME GABS!!!

😫 😫 😫 😨 😨

CECILY

UMMMM

OMG

THIS IS A LOT TO DIGEST 💜 💜 💜

GABRIELLE

Pri?

CECILY

I think her phone got taken away . . .

Overheard her telling Vishal in the hallway

She tried 2 tell me but I'm not talking 2 her right now

GABRIELLE

Ok

Everything feels so sad

🐻

CECILY

R u going to tell Colin it was u??

GABRIELLE

IDK

😳😳😳😳

CECILY

I gtg

GABRIELLE

🐻

CECILY

See u tomw

🩶🩶

Colin, Gabrielle

COLIN

U there?

GABRIELLE

Yup

COLIN

See if u can find out, k?

GABRIELLE

K, I'll try

From: Prianka Basak
To: Cecily Anderson, Gabrielle Katz
Subject: WAHHHHHH

Hi, guys—

My mom took my phone away because she saw what happened on the text with Victoria. That app really works! Also, Victoria's mom emailed my mom. And Mr. Carransey called me in. UGH. I am in so much trouble. I don't even know when I can get my phone back. I feel so lost without it. WAH. So sad over here.

xoxo Pri

Cecily, Gabrielle

CECILY

Pri doesn't even get that I'm mad @ her . . .

Doesn't she c how dumb it was 2 do that & how much she hurt V's feelings 😠 😠 😠 😠 😫 😫 😫 😫 🫨 🫨

Gabs, hello

R u there

GABRIELLE

I'm here . . .

IDK what 2 say.

It's all messed up

I'm scared of writing anything bc of my mom w/ that app!

😿 😿 😿

Ugh ok

Bye xox

♥♥

From: Gabrielle Katz
To: Colin Hayes
Subject: no subject

colin,

hey. i'm emailing you instead of texting bc my mom has that app to see my phone and i'm freaked out. meet me at my locker tomorrow before school and i will tell you who sent the note.

—gabby

From: Prianka Basak

To: Gabrielle Katz

Subject: Mad at me, too?

Gabs,

Are you mad at me, too? It was an accident.
I didn't mean to hurt Victoria's feelings. Can
we talk?

I miss you!

Pri

Cecily, Mara

C   M

CECILY

My friends turned crazy, I think . . . 😫 😢

MARA

?!?

Pri got in major trouble bc she was mean to Victoria on text

She got her phone taken away & promise u won't tell any1—Gabs is the 1 who sent note to Colin.

😲 😲 😵 😲

MARA

⁉️⁉️ OMG OMG OMG OMG

CECILY

PROMISE YOU WILL NOT TELL ANY1.

MARA

👄 👄 👄 = sealed.

CECILY

Com

E over after school tomw?

MARA

👍 👍 👍

MEMO

From: Mr. Carransey, Principal Yorkville Middle School
To: ALL SIXTH-GRADE STUDENTS, ALL SIXTH-GRADE PARENTS
Re: Valentine's Day Dance

Dear sixth graders and parents:

The Valentine's Day dance has been canceled. Students were warned about the consequences of their behavior, but the social cruelty continued. It's more than that—I see you when you are talking to one another, and sometimes you do not even lift your heads to talk face-to-face. Your eyes are glued to your phones. Do you value your phones more than social decency? Spend some time thinking about this.

Sincerely,
Edward Carransey
Principal
Yorkville Middle School

Be the change you want to see in the world.—Gandhi

Colin, Gabrielle

COLIN

R u sure bout that note?

GABRIELLE

Uh huh

COLIN

Doesn't make sense

We r just badminton partners

GABRIELLE

Trust me

COLIN

I don't like her tho . . .

GABRIELLE

So just forget about the note, k

COLIN

U r kinda weird . . .

GABRIELLE

Am not

GTG

Dear Diary,

I did another dumb thing. I can't even put it in writing. I think my mom is snooping. Everything feels terrible. I want to run away.

Love,
Gabby

Cecily, Mara

MARA

So much fun hangin w/ u yest 👏 👏 👏

CECILY

I KNOW

Good thing we r normal 1s in our groups so we can hang 👧👧 👧👧

MARA

Totally

Every1 is bonkers

👽 🐮 👽

But I have to tell u something . . .

Promise not to freak? 🙇 🙏

CECILY

Ummmm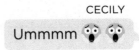

MARA

Sooo Gabby's locker is next to mine &
I heard her talking to Colin before 1st
period . . .

CECILY

Yeah 😲 😲

MARA

She told him u sent him an anonymous love
letter or something? 😲 😲 😲 😲 😲 😲
😲 😲 😲 😲

• • •

CECILY

What

Me?

R u sure you heard right

171

MARA

Yeah . . . It was like she didn't know what to say or something . . . Seemed SO SO SO weird 😵 😵 😵

CECILY

Ummm I am so confused

People r just getting weirder 😥 😥 😥 😥 😥

MARA

I KNOW 👽 👽 👽 👽 👽

CECILY

Let's run away 2gether 2 our own island or something 🥷 🗡 🥷 🗡

MARA

OK!!!! 👍 👍 👍 👊

CECILY

I am so embarrassed tho

I don't like Colin!!

We still have to play badminton together

What should I do??

😒 😔 😞 😣

MARA

Pretend u don't know . . . Just act normal
🐤🐤🐤

CECILY

UGH this is soo annoying

Does any1 care about getting the dance back 😫 😨 💃 👯 🧜 🤸 🎎

MARA

IDK

CECILY

I want to skip school 4ever

I am in a fight with Prianka

& now Colin thinks I like him

173

& tbh this is soooooo awkward

MARA

It'll be ok

Just hang w/ me

CECILY

M girls + C?

MARA

Hee hee

We don't even call ourselves that anymore

K, nighty night 😙 😙 😙

SWAK 😙 😙

From: Prianka Basak
To: Cecily Anderson
Subject: I MISS YOUUUUU

Hi, Cece,

I miss you so much. I don't know when I'm getting my phone back. Please talk to me, Cece. I wrote Victoria an apology letter. I need to tell you what happened at Bal Vihar on Sunday. I think Vishal wants to go out with me. What should I do? I really miss you. . . .

xoxo Pri

Prianka Basak's Sad Missing Her Phone Poetry Book

Poem 1
Prianka is sad
Her phone is gone
When will she get it back?
How does anyone survive without a phone?
I wish I knew

From: Gabrielle Katz
To: Prianka Basak
Subject: CAN YOU USE THE PHONE AT ALL??

Pri,

I'm writing this from computer lab. I really

need to talk to you in private. Can you use the phone? Like a landline? It is really important.

xo Gabs

READING LOG

V– Here are my reading log pages. So sorry again about that group text. I feel so bad for Auggie. Middle school is hard enough with a regular face, ya know? –G

I know—but even saying "regular face" sounds insensitive, to be honest. Thanks for apologizing. Here are my pages. —V

From: Prianka Basak
To: Gabrielle Katz
Subject: NO PHONES ALLOWED

gabs,

i'm not allowed to call/text/anything. i am only allowed on email to get school assignments, so even this is illegal. meet me in front of the cafeteria before 1st period tomorrow and we can talk. me and vishal are a real couple! omg. too bad I can't talk to him at all outside of school or bal vihar. BOO HOO.

smooches, pri

Cecily, Gabrielle

C G

CECILY

I am so so so mad at u btw

I figured u'd at least tell me urself what u did, but I had to hear from like 3 other peeps

GABRIELLE

I am so sorry, Cece

I wanted to tell him it was me

But at last second I froze & I was like "well, Cece can handle anything" so I said u

But I am so so sorry

DON'T CRYING CAT FACE ME!!!!!

WE ARE PAST EMOJIS RIGHT NOW

I don't like Colin

I don't like any boy right now

I need a break, ok

Please don't text me anymore

GABRIELLE

Please please please forgive me

I will do anything

CECILY

I SAID DON'T TEXT ME ANYMORE

Poem 2
We wish and wish and wish and wish
But some things don't come true
It is the way of life
Might as well get used to it

From: Gabrielle Katz
To: Colin Hayes
Subject: Hi

Dear Colin,

I need to tell you something. It was me who wrote the note. I don't know why I lied and said it was Cecily. I guess because you are badminton partners and it seemed believable and I got scared. I have liked you for a really long time. I guess that's all I have to say.

From, Gabby

Hi, Cece, I'm writing you this note because you said not to text you anymore, but you didn't say I couldn't pass you a note between classes. I am so so sorry about what I did. I don't have a good excuse, really, but I got scared. Can we please talk? xoxo Gabs

Dear Gabs, I know you're sorry. Thanks for apologizing. But honestly, I just can't deal with the drama right now. I'm still really mad and I think I just need a break from you and Pri for a bit. —Cece

Gabrielle, Victoria

VICTORIA

Gabby, r u there 🐱 🐱 😼 🙀

GABRIELLE

Yeah

Hi

VICTORIA

Just wanted to say that I saw u crying after school 2day by the bus line

I felt really bad but I didn't know what 2 say

So I'm texting u now 2 check in 🖤 💔 💝 🖤 💔 💝

GABRIELLE

Oh, thanx

That's really sweet of u

U r def the Summer of Yorkville

VICTORIA

R u ok

& YAY!

Summer is my fave char in WONDER!!!!!! "If you can get through middle school without hurting anyone's feelings, that's really cool beans."

GABRIELLE

Seriously

I guess my friends & I can't do that . . . Cecily is mad at me & Pri still doesn't have her phone but all she cares about is Vishal & I sent Colin that anonymous note & then I admitted it was me, & I haven't heard anything from him since & my mom said we are definitely moving this summer . . .

😠 😠 😳 😵 😨 😔 🥺

VICTORIA

Wow that was a long text

Longest text I've ever gotten

That is prob so dorky to say

6d 6d 6d 6d

GABRIELLE

LOL not dorky

😂 😂

VICTORIA

Maybe Colin doesn't know what 2 say

Boys r kinda slow LOL 😂 😂

GABRIELLE

LOL. Maybe

VICTORIA

It'll all work out 🤞🤞

GABRIELLE

U think? 😲

VICTORIA

Yes

Def

If u ever want 2 talk or uh text I'm here

GABRIELLE

LOL

Thanx, Victoria

💜 💜

Cecily, Mara

CECILY

So do u think I should write that email 2 the grade about putting our phones in Mr. Carransey's office 4 a day

MARA

I think it's a great idea 💡💡❗

CECILY

His secretary said she'd put out a box and just make sure all phones are labeled

I think it'll make a strong point

MARA

Def 👍

CECILY

I'm nervous—what if no1 does it? 😲 😳 😵

MARA

Well, send the email & then ask people to respond if they're gonna do it

Ya know

CECILY

Good idea 👍

From: Cecily Anderson
To: 6th Grade Students
Subject: Phones and texting

Dear classmates:

By now you have all heard that Mr. Carransey canceled the Valentine's Day dance because of social cruelty in the school. It is in the other grades, too, but mostly our grade. I thought we could all prove that we value each other more than our phones, by doing a phone drop. We'll all put our phones in a box in Mr. Carransey's office and leave them there overnight. Hopefully he will be pleased by this and realize that we are done with social cruelty and texting and social media, and he will reconsider having the dance. Please reply and let me know if you will be participating. Then I will provide instructions.

Sincerely,
Cecily Anderson, 6th grade rep

Cecily, Mara

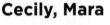

CECILY

OMG—have gotten so many responses

MARA

Everyone is gonna do it?

CECILY

I think so!

I'll give it a few more days

MARA

Yay we are totes getting our dance back 🐧
🐰🐧🐰

CECILY

YAAAAA 👏👏👏👏

~~~~~~~~~~~~~~~~~~~~~~~~~~~~~~~~~~~~~

Dear Diary,

Colin still hasn't responded about the note. Cecily isn't talking to me. I am embarrassed to bring it up to Pri. So embarrassed.

Love,
Gabby

~~~~~~~~~~~~~~~~~~~~~~~~~~~~~~~~~~~~~

PRIANKA

Guess who has her fone back???? 👏📱👏

GABRIELLE

Welcome back 🐧💃🐧💃

CECILY

Welcome back but I'm still not talking 2 either of u

GABRIELLE

Right, well, this is texting not talking 😂😂😂

CECILY

BLARGH 😠😠😠😠

GABRIELLE

Cece, I liked ur idea of the phone drop

PRIANKA

I liked it 2

CECILY

Thanks

GABRIELLE

How'd you get ur phone back, Pri?

Cecily HAS LEFT THE CHAT

Prianka, Gabrielle

GABRIELLE

Sheesh she's really not talking to us 🙅 🙅

PRIANKA

Guess not 😨 😨

GABRIELLE

Soooooo how'd u get it back???

PRIANKA

Well

Long story

Ready? ✎ ✎ ✎ ✎

GABRIELLE

Yesssss

PRIANKA

Well, my parents said I couldn't get it back until I realized what I'd done & how my words affect others so I was like, uhhhh . . .

But then I realized what I could do

In my meeting with Mr. Carransey I told him I could start a task force

Like a group

GABRIELLE

I don't get it 😮 😮

PRIANKA

Like we could have meetings and stuff 2 make sure every1 is being nice & using their phones for good

GABRIELLE

Ummmm ok sure 👍🏻👍🏻👏🏻👏🏻

PRIANKA

Isn't it genius

We r going 2 start in march!! 👏🏻👏🏻👏🏻

GABRIELLE

I guess?

PRIANKA

GABS, it is genius 😎😎😎

GABRIELLE

Congrats, Pri

U got ur phone back & u r helping humanity 2 . . . 🌍🌎🌏

YES YES YES!!!!! ☮ ☮ ☮ ☮ ☮ ☮

Reason #6 to stay in
Yorkville:
Sometimes we do the
wrong thing, but we
always fix it.

♡ xoxo

DEAR PRIANKA:
I GOT THESE LETTERS AT THE COMIC BOOK STORE. AREN'T THEY COOL? IT HELPS TO PASS THE TIME IN STUDY HALL. DO U THINK WE'LL GET THE DANCE BACK?
-VISHAL

Cece, Hope you go to your locker before lunch to see this note!!! I just walked by Mr. Carransey's office, and the box for phones is almost full! GO YOU! xoxo Mara

From: Colin Hayes
To: Gabrielle Katz
Subject: Note

Dear Gabby,

Thanks for telling me about the note. Sorry I forgot to write back for so long. It's cool that you like me.

—Colin

Prianka, Gabrielle

P G

GABRIELLE

What does that email mean??

PRIANKA

IDK

Guess he thinks it's cool

😎😎😎

Do u understand 👦👦🏃🏃?

Not really

Hee hee

😂😂😂

UGH

BYE

💗💗💗

Cece, I am so so so sorry about the whole thing with the note. Please forgive me. Meet me outside the cafeteria for lunch. I am so so sorry.
I love you. Gabs

MEMO

From: Mr. Carransey, Principal, Yorkville Middle School
To: ALL SIXTH-GRADE STUDENTS

Please meet in the auditorium after third period.

Thank you,
Edward Carransey
Principal
Yorkville Middle School

Be the change you want to see in the world.—Gandhi

Cecily, Mara

MARA

OMG, CECILY!

U did it

U got the dance back

CECILY

Well, we ALL did it

Every1 dropped their phones

The whole grade

MARA

I can't believe it

SO EXCITED THO

CECILY

Me too!!!!

Dear Cece,
Congrats on all your hard work on getting the dance back. I just want to say sorry again for the note thing. It was inexcusable. Please find with this note a bag of peanut m&ms. Your favorite. Please forgive me.
xoxo Gabs

BFFAE 4 REAL

CECILY

OK, u guys, thx 4 all the notes & emails & everything

I'm done being in a fight

🐧🐧 🐧🐧 🐧🐧 🐧🐧 🐧🐧

PRIANKA

4 real? 💙💙💙 💙💙

GABRIELLE

YEAH?? 💙💙💙💙💙💙💙💙💙💙💙💙💙💙

CECILY

I missed u guys

But here r new ground rules

READY?

PRIANKA
YUP ✔ ✔

GABRIELLE
YUPPPPPP ✔ ✔

CECILY
1. No texting fights
2. Make sure u know who u r group texting
3. No lying about secret admirer notes
4. No M girl bashing
5. Gabby is not allowed 2 move
6. We must have fun at the dance 2gether

GABRIELLE
WORKS 4 ME! ✔ ✔

PRIANKA
ME 2!!!!! ✔ ✔

Vishal, Prianka

VISHAL

So dance is back on . . .

PRIANKA

👀👀👀👀

VISHAL

R u allowed 2 go?

PRIANKA

✔️

VISHAL

Cool

PRIANKA

R u going?

VISHAL

Yea

V— Thanks for being so caring. —Gabby

♡ ♡ ♡

No problem. Glad you made up with your
friends. Can we hang at the dance? —V

♡ ♡ ♡ ♡

Definitely. Sorry I'm passing notes in
class, but I didn't want you to think
I was ignoring you.

Thanks! xoxo

DANCE GIRLZZZZZZZ

VICTORIA

What is every1 wearing 2 the dance 👗🧥👔👙👕👕👢👠👡👞👜👛👑👟🎩

PRIANKA

Black flare-y dress and silver flats 🐺🐺

CECILY

Kelly green dress w/ tie waist.

Silver flats w/ tiny heel! 👏

GABRIELLE

🙌🙌🙌

Pink & white polka-dot dress (trust me, vv cute!) & silver mini-heels

Guess we love silver!!

U?

VICTORIA

That all sounds amazing!!!

I think I'm going 2 wear this pale blue dress and—wait for it—silver platforms!!!

CECILY

K, it's official

We are now the Silver Girls! 🎉 🎉

GABRIELLE

YEAHHHHH 👊 👊 👊 👊

PRIANKA

Nice, Cece! 💪 💪 💪

VICTORIA

I LUV IT!!!!!!!! 😎 😎 😎 😎

From: Prianka Basak
To: Cecily Anderson, Gabrielle Katz
Subject: Re: Following my rules

ALL GOOD!

> **From:** Gabrielle Katz
> **To:** Cecily Anderson, Prianka Basak
> **Subject:** Re: Following my rules
>
> Agree! She's my reading log buddy. . . .

> > **From:** Cecily Anderson
> > **To:** Gabrielle Katz, Prianka Basak
> > **Subject:** Following my rules
> >
> > See, I am not starting a separate text to you guys without Victoria . . . I am emailing instead. So don't roll your eyes about the Silver Girls thing. I was just trying to be nice and make her feel included. And honestly, she's not that bad. xoxo

Dear Diary,

So I made up with my friends, finally. And Colin was nice about the note. Now all I need to figure out is how to dance with Colin at the Valentine's Day dance. Any ideas?

Love,
Gabby

Reason #7, #8, #9 to stay in Yorkville: Fireworks at Millbrook Pier on 4th of July, Memorial Day parade down Sullivan Street, the outstanding school system. ♡ xoxo

From: Victoria Melford
To: Kimberly Higgins, Nicole Landenor
Subject: Hiiii

Wish you could come to Yorkville Middle's Valentine's Day dance! I'll send pics and stuff. Miss you guys.

LUV,
Victoria

Dear Diary,

Well, I had my first-ever school dance. And guess what? It was actually fun! I danced with my friends the whole time. Well, we ate pizza, too, and drank soda. But we danced a ton! Colin talked to me, too, but we didn't dance together. No girls danced with boys. But that's okay. And guess what else? My mom said she's putting the moving plan on hold. I guess now all I need to worry about is if Colin likes me back. And what to do for my birthday and also the math midterm. I guess that is a lot to worry about. And now I'm tired. Bye for now.

Love,
Gabby

SQUAD BFFAE BEST GIRLS EVA

P C G

PRIANKA

I'm not being exclusive but I wanted 2 send a simple text 2 the 2 of u & say gnight & luv you guys & can we please be BFF forever?

GABRIELLE

OF COURSE

I LUV U GUYS

CECILY

YESSSSSS 😍😍😍😍😍😍😍😍😍😍😍

PRIANKA

 CPG 4EVA!!

GLOSSARY

2 to
2gether together
4 for
4eva forever
any1 anyone
BFF best friends forever
BFFAE best friends forever and ever
b-room bathroom
b/t between
c See
caf cafeteria
comm committee
comp computer
DEK don't even know
def definitely
diff different
disc discussion
fab fabulous
fac faculty
fave favorite
fone phone
fyi for your information
gtg gotta go

gn good night

gnight good night

hw homework

ICB I can't believe

IDC I don't care

IDK I don't know

IHNC I have no clue

IK I know

ILY I love you

ILYSM I love you so much

JK just kidding

K okay

L8r later

LMK let me know

lol laugh out loud

luv love

n e way anyway

nums numbers

obv obviously

obvi obviously

OMG oh my God

peeps people

pgs pages

plzzzz please

pos possibly

q question

r are

rlly really

sci science

sec second

sem semester

scheds schedules

SWAK sealed with a kiss

TBH to be honest

thx thanks

tm tomorrow

tmrw tomorrow

tomrw tomorrow

tomw tomorrow

totes totally

u you

ur your

vv very, very

w/ with

wb write back

w/o without

WIGO what is going on

whatev whatever

wut what

wuzzzz what's

Y why

ACKNOWLEDGMENTS

A million thank-yous going out to: Dave, Aleah, Hazel, all the Greenwalds, all the Rosenbergs, the BWL Library & Tech team, my fabulous editor, Maria, Rebecca, Katherine, Aurora, Amy, Erica, Bethany, Ann, Stephanie, and all the wonderful people at Katherine Tegen Books, superstar agent Alyssa, every single person who has ever read one of my books, and last but not least, all of my fabulous texting buddies. I love you all! XOXOXOXO

LISA GREENWALD lives in NYC 🍎 w/ her husband & 2 young daughters 👧 👧 👧 👧. She 💗s: 😎 📚 🏃 & 💈. Visit her 💻 @ www.lisagreenwald.com.

Don't miss Lisa Greenwald's next book!